GUINE

D1434177

GUINEA PIGS
ON THE GO

Vivian French
Illustrated by Clive Scruton

CollinsChildren'sBooks
An Imprint of HarperCollinsPublishers

First published in Great Britain by
CollinsChildren'sBooks 1997

3 5 7 9 8 6 4 2

CollinsChildren'sBooks is a division of
HarperCollins*Publishers* Ltd,
77-85 Fulham Palace Road,
Hammersmith, London W6 8JB

Printed and bound in Great Britain
by Caledonian International Book Manufacturing,
Glasgow G64

ISBN 0 00675258-6

CONTENTS

GUINEA PIGS ON THE GO

Mrs Gussie Guinea Pig peered at herself in the mirror and nodded.

"Yes," she said to herself. "I really am a very beautiful animal *and* I have four beautiful children. Or is it five?"

Mrs Gussie Guinea Pig was not good at counting. She became muddled after three, and even more muddled after four.

"Now, let me see," she said to herself.
"Minnie is one, and Winnie makes two.

And Millie and Tillie make two more.

And then there's Snuffler. But is that
four? Or five?"

Mrs Gussie Guinea Pig shook her head. "Never mind," she said to herself. "ALL my children are beautiful. And I shall take ALL of them to the fair. Even Snuffler." She sighed. "Even though he is *not* a good little guinea pig."

Mrs Gussie sighed again, and went downstairs.

Millie and Tillie and Minnie and Winnie were squeaking in the hallway.

"Mother! Mother! Mother! Snuffler's eaten all the potato peelings, and now we can't make a potato peelings pie to take to the fair."

There was a loud hiccup, and Snuffler skipped out of the kitchen.

"Snuffler!" said Mrs Gussie. "You are a *very naughty* boy!"

Snuffler began to snuffle. "But I was *so* hungry," he said. "I didn't *mean* to be naughty."

"That's what he always says," said
Millie to Tillie.

"He's a cry baby," said Tillie to Millie.
Mrs Gussie patted Snuffler's head.
"There there," she said. "Never mind."

"That's what she always says," said Minnie to Winnie.

"He's just a mummy's boy," said Winnie to Minnie.

Snuffler gave another loud hiccup. "Potato peelings are YUMMY!" he said, and followed Mrs Gussie back in to the kitchen. "Can I have some carrot tops?"

Outside in the hall Minnie and Winnie
and Millie and Tillie looked at each other.
"He's HORRIBLE!"
said Millie.

"He's GREEDY!" said Tillie.

"He's SPOILT!" said Winnie.

Minnie nodded. "Snuffler," she said, "needs to be taught a lesson!"

Winnie and Millie and Tillie stared at her. "HOW?"

Minnie scratched her ear. "Just watch me." she said. "I've got a plan."

"OK," said Winnie and Millie and Tillie.

Mrs Gussie Guinea Pig put on her best coat. Then she put on her best hat.

"Are you ready, piglets?" she called.

"Yes, Mother!" said Minnie and Winnie and Millie and Tillie.

"Where's little Snuffler?" asked Mrs Gussie anxiously.

Snuffler came trotting in. He was chewing hard and a dandelion leaf was tucked behind his ear.

"Snuffler, dear," Mrs Gussie said. "I do hope you haven't been in my store cupboard."

Snuffler snuffled. "But I was *so* hungry," he said.

Millie and Tillie snorted, but Minnie patted Snuffler's head.

"DEAR little Snuffler," she said. "I'm sure he didn't mean to be naughty."

Snuffler looked surprised. So did Mrs Gussie.

"There, there," said Minnie. "And I'm sure Mother will let us look after you at the fair."

Mrs Gussie beamed at her four children. (Or was it five? She could never quite remember.)

Mrs Gussie loved fairs, and if the children could look after each other, she could go driving on the dodgems. She could shoot plastic ducks on the shooting range. She could throw rubber rings over exciting prizes...

"Of *course* you may look after Snuffler, Minnie dear. But do be very careful, and be sure to stay together."

Snuffler was feeling worried. Minnie and Winnie and Millie and Tillie were looking very pleased with themselves.

"But I want to go with my mumsy," he said in his best little-pig snuffle.

"Not today, dear," said Mrs Gussie firmly, and she swept them up the path. At the entrance to the fair Mrs Gussie stopped to give Minnie and Winnie and Millie and Tillie their pocket money.

"Look after Snuffler's money for him," she said.

"I'll look after everyone's, Mother," said Minnie.

"Well!" said Mrs Gussie. "How kind of you, Minnie dear."

"What sensible children I have," she thought.

Minnie is up to something," thought Winnie and Millie and Tillie.

"Bother!" thought Snuffler.

"You may have three rides each,"
Mrs Gussie said, "and a toffee apple
and a candy floss and a sticky lolly and
a hot dog. Oh, and a fizzy drink. But
you must be back here at six o'clock."

Snuffler was still worried. Minnie and
Winnie kept winking at each other, and
Millie and Tillie kept giggling.

"I want to go with YOU, Mumsy!" he
snuffled.

Mrs Gussie shook her head. She could
see the dodgems and she was longing to
have a ride. "Off you go, my dears!"

As soon as Mrs Gussie had bustled off Snuffler sat down. "I want my toffee apple!" he said. "I want it NOW!"

Minnie nodded. "Of course, Snuffler dear."

Winnie and Tillie and Millie stared at her. Then they nodded too. "Of course you can, Snuffler. Come along!"

They went straight to the toffee apple stall.

"Five toffee apples, please," Minnie said.

"But I don't want mine now," said Millie.

"They're not for you." Minnie picked up the toffee apples. "They're *all* for Snuffler."

"WINK! WINK!" Snuffler bounced up and down. Winnie and Millie and Tillie glared at Minnie.

"Shhh!" said Minnie. "Wait and see!"

Snuffler crunched up the last of the toffee apples.

"Now can we go on a ride?" Millie asked.

Minnie shook her head. "Candy floss for Snuffler," she said.

Winnie and Millie and Tillie stood up.

"He's HORRIBLE!" said Millie.

"He's GREEDY!" said Tillie.

"He's SPOILT!" said Winnie.

"Sshhh!" hissed Minnie. "Do you want to teach him a lesson or not?"

Winnie and Millie and Tillie nodded.

"Then we've got to buy him some candy floss!"

"WINK! WINK!" said Snuffler and bounced up and down.

Snuffler ate five large candy flosses. Then he ate five huge sticky lollies. Then he ate five hot dogs.

Winnie and Millie and Tillie were fed up.

"It's not working," said Winnie.

"He's *still* horrid," said Millie.

"I want to go on the rollercoaster!" said Tillie.

Minnie nodded. "Oh, we will. But first I think Snuffler wants a fizzy drink. *Five* fizzy drinks."

"Don't want a drink," said Snuffler.

"Oh yes you DO," said Minnie.

After five fizzy drinks Snuffler was very very quiet.

"Want my mumsy," he said feebly.

"Now," said Minnie, "we're all going to go on the rollercoaster!"

"Don't want to go on the rollercoaster," said Snuffler.

"OH YES YOU DO!" said Minnie and Winnie and Millie and Tillie.

They had three rides each on the rollercoaster.

After the first ride Snuffler promised not to be horrid.

After the second ride he promised not to be greedy.

After the third ride he promised not to be spoilt.

When Minnie suggested they all had one last ride Snuffler burst into tears.

"AHA!" said Minnie. "Time to go home!"

Mrs Gussie was waiting for them at the fair gate. She had won four toffee apples, five sticky lollies, seven bottles of fizz and forty-two coconuts.

"Now my dears," she said. "Shall we share them out."

"Snuffler's feeling poorly, Mother," said Minnie. "I don't think he'll want anything."

"YES I DO!" said Snuffler. "I can eat ALL of those!"

And he did.

GUINEAS GO CAMPING

Minnie and Winnie and Millie and Tillie were sitting in a row by the front door. Their back packs were beside them and their tent was rolled up neatly.

"Isn't Auntie here YET?" asked Minnie.

"No, dear," said Mrs Gussie Guinea Pig. "But I'm sure she'll be here soon."

Snuffler came marching into the hall. He was carrying an umbrella and pulling a large bag of carrots behind him.

"I'm coming too!" he announced.

"OH NO YOU'RE NOT!" said Minnie and Winnie and Millie and Tillie.

Snuffler began to wail. Mrs Gussie patted his head.

"There, there," she said. "You can go camping when you're bigger."

"Not with us, he can't," said Minnie.

"That's right!" said Winnie and Millie and Tillie.

Mrs Gussie Guinea Pig shook her head sadly. She loved all her five children (or was it four? She was never quite certain. Mrs Gussie was NOT good at counting). She found it very difficult to understand why the girls didn't want dear little Snuffler to do whatever they did.

"I want to go toooo," Snuffler wailed.

Mrs Gussie patted his head again. "There, there. Run along and look in the cupboard. I think you might find a nice slice of lettuce pie."

Snuffler stopped wailing and trotted off to the kitchen.

The door bell rang. Minnie and Winnie and Millie and Tillie all jumped up and Minnie opened the door. Auntie was standing outside.

"Well, well, well!" she said. "Are all my jolly little campers ready?"

"Yes!" said Minnie and Winnie and Tillie and Millie.

"Uffle!" said Snuffler as he hurried back, his mouth full of lettuce pie. "Uffle um mump!"

"Goodness me," said Auntie. "What a big boy you are now! And are you coming with us?"

"NO!" shouted Minnie and Winnie and Tillie and Millie.

"YES!" shouted Snuffler.

"How SWEET!" sniffed Mrs Gussie
fondly.

Minnie dropped her back pack on the
ground. "If he's coming I'm not going,"
she said.

"What's all this?" asked Auntie. "I'm sure the little fellow won't be any trouble."

"He will," said Minnie. "He thinks he's so clever."

"He's greedy," said Winnie.

"He's horrible," said Millie.

"He's spoilt," said Tillie.

Auntie laughed a jolly laugh.

"He'll be fine with me," she said. "Run along and pack your things, little fellow, and we'll be off."

Snuffler let out a loud squeak and rushed up the stairs. Mrs Gussie bustled after him.

Minnie and Winnie and Tillie and Millie sat down on their back packs with a groan.

Mrs Gussie popped Snuffler's things into a bag. Snuffler snatched it and scuttled downstairs as fast as he could.

"I'm ready!" he said.

"Good!" said Auntie. "My van's outside. Let's be off!"

Mrs Gussie waved them goodbye.

"What a wonderful family I have," she thought to herself. "Four beautiful children! Or is it five? I never do seem to be able to remember."

She went on waving until they had turned the corner. Then she went inside to put her feet up.

"I hope Snuffler is a *good* boy," she said as she settled down. "He is sometimes just a teensy weensy bit naughty."

She yawned. "But I'm sure Auntie will look after him." And Mrs Gussie Guinea Pig closed her eyes and went to sleep.

Snuffler was very good for the first mile.

For the second mile he made "Yah boo! I'm so clever!" faces at Minnie until she pinched him. Then he burst into tears and Auntie had to give him a carrot to cheer him up.

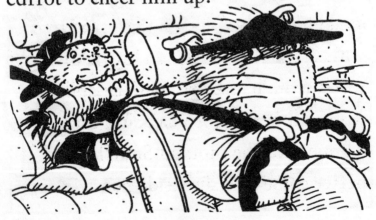

At the end of the third mile Winnie discovered that Snuffler had undone her back pack and eaten all her dandelion biscuits.

At the end of the fourth mile Snuffler said he felt sick. They had to stop and wait while Millie fetched him a drink of water from a stream. Snuffler spilt the water all over Tillie's sleeping bag, so Auntie said she thought Snuffler had better come and sit beside her.

They arrived at the camp site as the sun was setting.

"What quiet girls!" Auntie said as she parked the van.

"We've been making plans," Minnie said. She gave Snuffler a dark stare.

Snuffler looked anxious.

"Ho ho ho!" said Auntie. "Now – let's put these tents up!"

Auntie's tent went up first.

"Can I have this one?" Snuffler asked. "I don't want to share. I want my OWN tent."

Auntie laughed her jolly laugh. "You share with your sisters, young fellow," she said. "They'll look after you."

Minnie was looking more cheerful.
"That's right!" she said. "We'll look
after you."

Winnie winked at Millie and Tillie.

Millie and Tillie winked back.

After supper Snuffler didn't want to
go to bed. Minnie and Winnie and
Millie and Tillie washed and cleaned
their teeth and jumped into their
sleeping bags. Snuffler sat in front of
the camp fire and refused to move.

"I'm not tired," he said.

"Come along, come along," said Auntie.

"I want to go to bed out here," said Snuffler.

"But the fire will go out and you'll be cold," said Auntie.

"Snuffler!" Minnie called. "Would you like us to tell you a story?"

"There!" said Auntie. "Who's a lucky boy?" And she picked Snuffler up and popped him in the tent.

Minnie told Snuffler the first story. She told him about a terrible tiger that tiptoed among the rustling bushes looking for little guinea pigs. When it found them it ate them VERY VERY slowly, beginning with their noses.

Snuffler squeaked loudly and wriggled down his sleeping bag.

Winnie told the next story. She told
Snuffler about a slimy worm that lived
in the long whispering grass. It had an
ENORMOUS mouth, and it ate little
guinea pigs VERY VERY slowly,
beginning with their toes.

Snuffler snuffled and hid his head
under his pillow.

Millie told Snuffler about a giant ghostly guinea pig that hid behind the dark creaking trees. At night it crept here and there looking for little guinea pigs, and when it found them it ate them VERY VERY slowly, beginning with their ears.

Snuffler snuffled louder.

Tillie told Snuffler about the most horrible monster of all. It sniffled and snorted. When it smelt little guinea pigs it slithered out and gobbled them up VERY VERY FAST, all in one gulp.

Snuffler began to make a very strange noise indeed.

"*Poor* little Snuffler," said Minnie, and she winked at Winnie and Millie and Tillie. "I think you need your mumsy. I think you'd better run and tell Auntie that you want to go home NOW!"

Snuffler didn't move.

"Snuffler?" Minnie peered at him. "Snuffler, aren't you frightened?"

She lifted up the pillow. "Oh," she said.

"What is it?" asked Winnie.

"He's snoring!" said Minnie.

Minnie and Winnie and Millie and Tillie sat up in their sleeping bags.

"What shall we do now?" asked Winnie.

"We'll have to put up with him," said Millie.

Tillie was shivering. "Can you hear something?" she asked.

All four little guinea pigs sat quite
still and listened. The could hear the
bushes rustling and the grass
whispering. They could hear the trees
creaking in the wind. And they could
hear something sniffling and snorting
and it was very, very close.

"Oooooooh!" gasped Minnie and Winnie and Millie and Tillie, and they leapt out of their sleeping bags and rushed out of their tent.

"Auntie Auntie! There's a monster sniffling and snorting and it's going to gobble us up!"

Auntie sighed.

"You'd better bring your sleeping bags into my tent," she said.

In the morning Snuffler was the first up.

"Wakey wakey!" he squeaked.

Auntie yawned loudly. "Did you sleep well?"

"YES!" said Snuffler. He bounced into Auntie's tent. "Minnie and Winnie and Millie and Tillie told me EVER such exciting stories, and then I went to sleep." He jumped on Minnie and Winnie and Millie and Tillie to wake them up. "Can I have my own tent again tonight?"

Minnie and Winnie and Millie and Tillie looked at each other.

"No!" they said.

"Oh," said Snuffler. He put his head on one side. "I think perhaps you OUGHT to stay with Auntie," he said, "just in case the horrible monster comes back and frightens you again!"

Minnie and Winnie and Millie and Tillie stared at him.

"Yah boo! I'm so clever!" said Snuffler, and he sniffled and snorted and snorted and sniffled until it was time for breakfast.